Lake Erie Sea Monster

Bill J. Shortridge

DEDICATION

This book is dedicated to Jolene, Kathryn, Laura and Mat. They are some of the most creative people I know.

CONTENTS

ACKNOWLEDGMENTS

I want to acknowledge all of the people who looked on the Great Lakes and have experienced the unexplained movements and twilight activities on the Great Lakes and from these experiences some amazing stories have evolved.

1. THE MONSTER AND THE WAR

The Oniare (Own-yar-eh) is a dragon-like horned water serpent of the Erie, from the "Cat" Tribe. Their legends say that it lurks in the Great Lakes in order to capsize canoes and eat people. The Sea Serpent, Lake Monster and the Lake Erie Sea Monster (L.E.S.M.) has had many names. In the early 1800's the creature was seen in an open field and it was named Bessie because it's head resembled a cow. And some of the old timers of the day called it "Old Bess".

The Lake Erie Monster has had many sightings over the years. Some of the earliest were made by the Indians. They noted in their tales that the creature of the lake could be seen best at a full moon swimming close to South Bass Island.

The effects of the creature were noted in the log of a British officer during the Great Lake Battle during the War of 1812. The officer wrote, "As the battle was reaching the highest level of fighting, a seaman called me to the lower regions of the ship. Once I arrived I could see the horns of the beast sticking through the hull. The ship was shaking as the creature tried to set itself free. Once released, the water started pouring in and the ship began to sink." There were no other sightings for sometime after that encounter.

There are various opinions on how "Old Bess" came to be and why she stays in the Great Lake area of Lake Erie. The best explanation is that she is a carryover from the dinosaur age. As a monster, she has the ability to think and reason far better then her dinosaur cousins and learned how to survive the harsh elements. Some say she went to the southern islands where it was warmer and lived there for hundreds of years. After the planet warmed up, she moved north. She does hibernate during cold winter months and sometimes goes south for the winter.

"Old Bess" has been thought to be a killer since the days of the Indians and the War of 1812. When you are on the lake and your boat suddenly moves and shakes and the hair stands up on the back of your neck, you can be sure that you have just encountered "the ancient sea monster". I would quickly head for shore, if I were you.

2 THE CREATURE

There are so many questions surrounding this creature. What do we need to know about this creature? How big is she? Is she really a killer? Does she eat children under the age of 10? Where has she been seen and where does she live?

It has long been noted that she has not eaten anyone from the United States' side of Lake Erie. However, on the Canadian side of the Lake, there have been reports of people being eaten.

"Old Bess" has been around since the time of the dinosaurs and some say she is one. This could be, but we do not know for sure. There was an eye witness account in the year of 1789 that was logged in the Lake Erie historical records that claims she was 15 feet tall, 25 feet long, and weighed about 2,000 pounds (1 ton).

Over the past 200 years, even more facts have been gathered about the creature. It's said that her teeth are razor sharp and she can devour a Chinese carp in no time at all. She is solid and her skin is a rhino type and it's very tough. She can stay under water for hours and hours at a time. She is also very active at night, almost like a hippo. She particularly likes the light of the full moon. The creature also likes to get out of the water and lay in a nice, sunlit, clear area away from people.

The questions about this creature can never be totally answered without more information. Unless we ever have an opportunity to observe this creature more closely, there is so much we will never know. So, be on the lookout and report any sights to your Natural History office.

3 The Girl and the Monster

The Native Americans named the Cuyahoga River the "crooked river". The river flows south, then north at around the Indian "Signal Tree", the river flows and dumps into Lake Erie.. The signal tree is an old Bur Oak tree which still stands today. The Indians had to carry their canoes from the southern rivers edge down to other rivers to keep going south. The year was 1763, the monster would swim upstream on the Cuyahoga river to catch fish, that were in the river in abundance. Then the monster would rest down around the Indian signal tree before heading back to the lake. During this time there were Indian villages around this area and Chief Netawatwees was the leader of the Delaware tribe. In this tribe was a little girl, her name was Mary Campbell. She was adopted by the Chief and who took very good care of her. One day as the monster slept by the rivers bank, she was awaken by the sound of a person playing a bone flute. The monster was so amazed by the sound, she had to check it out. Then she saw the pretty red headed little girl who was playing the flute. She was beautiful in her leather clothing and had pretty colorful beads woven into her clothing. The sight and sounds put the monster in a daze. She watched her for about an hour before silently moving back into the river and swimming off. The monster came back again and again to the very same spot, but could not find her. But, she never forgot her music and her beauty.

4 Flip the Ship

The Lake Erie Sea Monster is very famous around the Great Lakes. Schools have monster mascots, drinks are named after the monster, T-shirts have monster art work and other items are inspired from these stories.

The year was 2017 and the place was the east side of Cleveland. It was December and Old Bess was out hunting for fish on the Lake Erie. She had not hibernated yet. A ship captain spotted her off the harbor and did not want to send his ship back into the lake. He heard reports how dangerous it could be with the monster around. She usually goes to her cave on the South Bass Island around the first of each year and emerges on March 20. Her timing is amazing. She heads for the island when the snow, wind, and temperatures become extreme.

Old Bess is drawn to the area around the

Breakwater Lighthouse. She has fond memories of this area. Back in 1884, a major wave capsized a barge close to the lighthouse. At least, everyone thought it was a wave. The schooner-rigged barge, the *John T. Johnson*, was attempting to make harbor off of the east pier when Bessie flipped it. The rescue efforts were historic for Cleveland, but Old Bess was not seen through all the commotion. She was just having a little fun.

5 SMALL TOWN

The village of Nottingham, Ohio was located in Euclid Township in Cuyahoga County. It was one of the strings of villages along the railroad running east from Cleveland. Nottingham became a part of Cleveland in 1912.

You might have heard about the event that happened that year in this small town. The village of Nottingham was taken over by the city of Cleveland. The town was in a turmoil and was very upset. The village did not want to be taken over by the large city. The railroad ran right through Nottingham going east from the city. The village people shut the railroad down for a week in protest. During that time, the village made such a loud noise that Old Bess could hear it. She came close to the shore and could hear the people yelling and screaming. It was at sunset and she saw 5 local men coming toward her. She let out a sound that made the men shutter and run for their lives. After she saw what was going on, she went back into the lake and swam off.

The stories these men told grew more amazing year by year. The local people did let the city take over the village, but not until the Sea Creature had some fun and shocked the men. She had to keep her distance over the years, because some of her interactions with people were not always positive. When people usually approached the monster, they were afraid and would not take the time to get to know her.

6 BIG WAVES

In 1882 and 1942, it was the time of the Great Waves on Lake Erie. Old Bess was almost swept away during those tragic events. Some might remember, but most would need to read history books about the Great Waves. If you bring up the Great Waves in conversation today, many would say that it did not happen and possibly call you crazy. It did happen as sure as the Ice Age formed the Great Lakes. The high waves came on a clear, sunny, and calm day without any notification. No one was ready for what they saw. The waves brought boats, logs, and anything close to land up onto the shore. These items covered the shore line all over the Lake Erie.

Old Bess was out in the middle of the lake when an intense storm blew up. There was hail and high winds and then it happened, a gigantic water spout appeared. It sucked water up into the air hundreds of feet. And when it stopped the major waves were created by the water being let down again. The Sea Creature was swept away by the powerful wind and carried along for miles.

She dove down into the water to escape its power and broke free. She was then able to swim to shore. She dragged herself onto shore and was totally exhausted. It was days before she would swim far from the shore.

The year this event happened was 1882. She was on land when the big wave came in 1942 and was not effected. She still remembers the great waves and wonders if it will ever happen again. Even today, when a storm is on the lake, Old Bess takes care to get to shore as soon as possible.

7 THE FUTURE

The future for the Lake Erie Sea Monster is bright. The water today is so much clearer and cleaner. But the monster does not like it when people just throw their trash into the water. It makes the monster very angry. So, we can all do our part in keeping the Great Lakes great by helping to keep it clean for the monster, fish and people.

Does the monster have friends? The answer is yes. Since it is a monster, you would think everything would run, swim or hide from the beast, but that is not true. There are very large fish in the Great Lakes that are called sturgeon. They can get as large as 10 feet long and weigh up to 300 pounds. Now that is a large fish and the monster has seen many fish this size. Now a school of large sturgeon became friends with the monster in a very strange way. "Old Bess" got into a terrible situation with an old ship's rigging laying on the bottom of the lake. As the monster swam by the old ship looking for fish to catch, it got caught in the ropes. It was a desperate situation and almost a fatal one. The school of large sturgeon were around that area and could hear the monster moaning and trying to escape. So, the sturgeons went close and with their suction like mouth started to remove the ropes. Once the monster was free, it promised never to eat another sturgeon and swore to be friends forever. It was one of the happiest days when the monster became friends with the sturgeons. If the monster sees anyone one fishing for sturgeons, it will break the fisherman's line quicker than you can say "fried catfish".

Appendices:

Lake Erie Sea Monster Poem

From where you came a mystery hidden,
And on your back no one has ridden.

On beach and land spending your time,
And sometimes interacting with the human kind.

Not that you meant to cause such a scare,
When humans see you they are bound to stare.

But thru all your travels the Lake you did find,
Lake Erie is your home with peace of mind.

The monster is a stir and swimming so fast,
The Lake Erie Sea Monster is home at last.

Lake Erie Facts

- Length : 241 miles
- Breadth: 57 miles
- Entire Coast: 871 miles
- Ohio's Coast: 312 miles
- Ohio's Public Access Miles: ~56.2 miles
- Average Depth: 62 feet
- Maximum Depth: 210 feet
- Volume: 127.7 trillion gallons
- Outlets: Niagara River and Welland Canal
- Monsters: Lake Erie Sea Monster
- Ship wrecks: 2,000

ABOUT THE AUTHOR

Whenever you have a large expanse of water and people around, stories arise about sea creatures and monsters. I am interested in the stories of the Lake Erie Sea Monster. I have visited the Great Lakes many times and have heard different stories of the Monster.

I have always wanted to write a book. I struggled to read and comprehend what I read when I was going thru school. I would read only the words and not the thoughts behind the words. God healed me of this and I read very well today.

Manufactured by Amazon.ca
Bolton, ON